D1553501

Written and Illustrated by
Christopher Stinton

ISBN: 9798699211838

To my boys, Thomas and Christopher Jr.
And to all families with special needs, your
inspiring strength can slay the mightiest of
dragons.

CHAPTERS

CHAPTER ONE

PIZZA FOR BREAKFAST

"Jump! Tommy! Jump!" Chris shouted, standing on top of the breakfast table.

Tommy planted his bare feet on a squeaky chair. He was supposed to leap onto the table with Chris and I-doll.

"Boy, you better jump quick!" I-doll yelled. The little, wooden doll stood on Chris's shoulder.

"The floor is burning, hot lava!" Chris cried, pointing to the floor. "Your chair's gonna' melt!"

Blowing the brown hair out of his eyes, Tommy looked down. There was no burning, hot lava – just a dirty floor covered in crumbs from the pizza they ate last night – and a couple of slices from breakfast.

He didn't care much for pretending the floor was hot lava, but jumping all over the furniture, Tommy lived for that. Tommy measured the distance from the chair to the table. One, two, three, four, five, six, maybe seven pizza slices across. It was quite a leap, even for him.

"Brother, hurry! Your chair's melting!" Chris cried as he fixed his helmet to see better. He never took that helmet off, except to eat.

With a deep breath, Tommy bent his legs, leaned forward, and jumped...

His toes grabbed the edge of the table.

But it wasn't enough.

Tommy wobbled and fell backwards!

Snatch! Chris grabbed Tommy's arm and pulled him onto the table.

"I've got you, brother!"

"Phew, that was a close one!" said I-doll as he hopped from Chris's shoulder to Tommy's shoulder.

Tommy touched his chin with his fingers – his way of thanking Chris and I-doll for saving him from falling into the burning, hot lava.

"You're welcome, brother," said Chris.

I-doll high-fived Tommy. "Good job using your hand gesture to thank us, boy," I-doll told Tommy. "You picked that up quickly."

Tommy smiled – then heard something crack below his feet.

Snap! Crack!

Tommy, Chris, and I-doll looked down at the table and then at each other.

"Oh, dragon farts," Chris mumbled.

The legs of the table snapped. *Snap! Crack! Bang! Crash!*

A moment later, the dust settled.

Tommy giggled as he sat up on the collapsed table.

"Oh, boy," I-doll cried. "We turned the table into firewood."

"Hurry, c'mon, lift it up," Chris told Tommy. "Maybe we can fix it before-"

"What happened to my table!" Mother stomped over to the two boys and the little doll with beaming eyes.

Chris brushed the dust from his pants. "Mother, we're sorry. We-"

"What did I tell you boys about jumping all over the furniture?"

I-doll took a deep breath and acted his heart out.

"Oh, but kind mother," I-doll pleaded, "we were just pretending the floor was hot lava. It is so much fun. Did you do something with your hair? You look so beautiful this morning."

But mother didn't fall for I-doll's charm. "Don't try to butter me up, I-doll," said mother, waving her finger at him.

"Chris, you're too old and big to be

jumping on the furniture," mother said, glaring at Chris. "I really need you to set a good example for Tommy. Your brother needs all the good examples he can get."

Tommy jumped up and hugged his mother. In fact, he lifted her off the floor with his mighty strength.

"Tommy, my goodness!" mother cried. "You're getting too strong for your own good."

"Alright, boys," said mother. "You need to hurry, you're both going to be late for school... I-doll, help Tommy get ready. Uncle Rick's taking him to the island today."

"Yes, ma'am!" I-doll nodded and turned to Tommy. "Tommy, let's go find your book... and your shoes... and your pants."

Tommy shot up and dashed to his bedroom. He almost forgot all about his book... almost.

"And I-doll, when you get back," mother said, "you get to help me fix the table. I'm having guests over later."

"Well, lucky me," I-doll mumbled.

Chris sighed. "I wish my school was on an island like Tommy's school," he told his mother.

"I know, sweetie," said mother. "But like I said, that school has special teachers to work with Tommy, and it's safer."

"I know. It's just cool that he gets to ride on the ferryboat there every morning." Chris frowned. "And that mountain his school sits near, did you know that's a sleeping volcano? A friend of mine told me that. I didn't know volcanos could sleep!"

"I know." Mother cringed. "But it's what's best for Tommy. Now, are you ready to go?"

"Almost," Chris said. "Our teacher wanted us to bring in something special to share with the class."

Chris darted to his messy bedroom, grabbed an item wrapped in cloth, and returned to his mother.

"I'm going to take this," Chris said, unwrapping the item. "Well, what's left of it."

Inside was the handle of a shattered sword.

"It's the sword I used to chop off the wings of Frosty the Ice Dragon," Chris told his mother. "Right before The Fire Queen broke it."

"Just be careful with it, sweetie," mother said.

"Mother, this thing couldn't cut the beard off a troll. Have you made me a new sword yet?"

"No, sweetie, not yet. I've been busy," she said. "Now get going. You're going to be late. And what's taking your brother so long?"

●●●

Tommy tiptoed across the many books

that cluttered his bedroom floor. In the center of his bedroom stood a perfectly stacked tower of books – the most important books.

Tommy slid a book from the top of the stack and opened it up on the floor… for the one hundredth time.

His finger dragged across the raised title of the book; *A Book of Wizards*. Tommy gently turned each stiff page, making sure they were all there.

"Boy, you really love that book, don't you?" asked I-doll as he hopped over and planted his tiny bum next to Tommy.

Tommy turned the next page and pointed to a drawing of an old man and waited for I-doll to read it to him… for the one hundredth time.

I-doll giggled. He didn't have much for a face – just two lines carved into his pointy head that made a T-shape – almost like a knight's helmet.

"Alright boy, one more time," I-doll told Tommy. "And then, you bring home a different book from school."

Tommy smiled, but he wasn't making any promises.

Although I-doll didn't have a throat, he cleared it anyway and took a deep breath.

"That's a wizard," I-doll said, pointing to the page with the old man. "Some of them live for hundreds of years – maybe thousands! Many of them have pointy hats and long beards."

I-doll pointed with his tiny hand at the long stick the wizard was holding in the picture. "That's a staff. It helps the Wizards to control magic, and wizards use magic to cast spells, or create special powers – all kinds of crazy stuff. And the source of the magic; comes from Dragon Stones."

Tommy turned the page, and then turned back to the page with the wizard again. He pointed to the old man with the staff – again.

"No more, boy," I-doll giggled.

"Tommy! I-doll! Let's go!" mother shouted from the other room. "You're going to be late!"

Tommy slammed the book shut, grabbed his green cloak, and ran out of the bedroom.

I-doll's tiny feet scampered behind. "Boy! You forgot your pants!"

CHAPTER TWO

UNDER THE SHADY TREE

Tommy's school rested on a quiet island across the narrow sea. Much like a castle, the school's stone towers stretched high into the sky. A proud and mighty wall of stone surrounded his entire school with only one way in and one way out.

Near the walls, a small creek splashed through some trees and rocks.

"Alright, boy. One more time," I-doll told Tommy.

Smiling, Tommy placed a tiny boat made of sticks into the creek.

I-doll hopped on it. He held on tightly

as the stick-boat floated and rocked through the splashing water.

"Ahh! Boy!" I-doll screamed. "I don't want to get wet again!"

The stick-boat zipped down a small waterfall and crashed into a rock.

I-doll flew through the air and bounced into a small patch of grass.

"Oh, my head," I-doll cried as Tommy came running over.

Tommy picked up I-doll and put him on his shoulder.

Gong! Gong! Large bells rang in the tall tower of Tommy's school.

"School's starting, boy," I-doll told Tommy. "I really wish I could go with you. But I'm just a 'distraction', they say."

Tommy gave I-doll a tiny high-five before placing him back on the ground.

"You be good, boy," I-doll said. "I'll see you after school."

Tommy smiled. He turned and dashed into his school. A large steel door slammed down behind him.

●●●

Morning had passed. The bells in the school tower rang once again. *Gong! Gong! Gong!*

The clanging rattled the trees and mountains, echoed through the hallways, and rang into Tommy's ears.

Three rings, Tommy thought. *That*

means it's time to go outside.

After glancing through his wizard book again, Tommy slammed the book shut and shoved it into one of the large pockets inside his cloak. He checked his other pockets. Sometimes he'd forget what was inside each of them.

One pocket had a few pancakes from last week. One had a pizza crust from yesterday. Most of the time, there was food inside of his pockets, and of course, his book.

Tommy jumped up in the middle of his classroom and ran to the exit. The other kids in his class had already lined up at the door.

Tommy's teacher stood over by the exit, Miss Egghead, or at least that was what the other kids called her.

Tommy wasn't sure what her actual name was, but it sounded something like that.

"Break time, kids," said Miss Egghead, clearing her throat. "Behave. Play nice. And for the one hundredth time, don't climb the walls. The walls are there to keep us safe."

One of the kids in front of Tommy giggled quietly.

"Hehe, 'play nice'," the kid snorted like a pig. "That's no fun."

Tommy burst outside with the other kids, but he didn't follow any of them. As usual, he ran alone through a grassy field with the sun sparkling through the clouds above.

In the corner of the large field, Tommy stopped at a tall and proud tree. Past the tree, the large stone walls stretched into the sky.

The shady tree comforted Tommy. He laid back against the rough bark and slowly slid down onto his bum. It was like getting a back scratch from a tree.

And once again, Tommy took out *The Book of Wizards* from his cloak and flipped through each page.

Tommy froze. Three shadows suddenly creeped over him.

"Hey, dummy!" a familiar voice snorted.

Tommy looked up. Three beefy kids glared down at him.

"Yeah, I'm talking to you, dummy. My name's Trent," said the middle kid. He then pointed to the two kids behind him. "These are my goons, Boon and Foon, and we noticed you were sitting under our tree here."

Tommy went back to his book, flipping the pages. He didn't know what Trent was talking about.

"Dummy? Can you hear me in there?" Trent snorted again at Tommy. "Dummy, why won't you look at me when I talk to you?"

Tommy ignored him while Boon and Foon giggled in the background.

Trent growled and snatched the *Book of Wizards* from Tommy's hands and dangled it above.

"What's this?" Trent asked. "A stupid book? Can you even read? Why don't you play with the other kids instead of reading a stupid book?"

Tommy jumped for his book, but Trent was much taller.

"You're so weird," Trent snapped. "You can't talk. You sit by yourself all the time. What's your deal? Are you just stupid?"

Boon and Foon giggled.

Tommy stopped jumping. He stared blankly out to the grassy field, thinking about what his brother would do, what I-doll would do, what a knight would do.

"I got an idea," said Trent. The awful boy held up *The Book of Wizards* in front of Tommy's face.

With an annoying grunt, Trent ripped the book in half.

"Maybe now, you'll get yourself a friend, dummy," Trent snarled.

Tommy's face tightened and turned bright red. He lunged forward and tackled Trent to the ground.

Thud!

Boon and Foon gasped.

"Someone, help!" Trent squealed. He pushed Tommy off of him. "Ugh! Get off of me, dummy!"

Scared and frozen, Tommy sat there in the grass. He felt unsure about what he just did.

Miss Egghead came running over.

"What happened?" she asked, helping Trent off the ground.

"It was Tommy!" Trent shouted as he held his side, pretending to be hurt. "We were just playing over here by the tree! He went crazy. He ripped his book in half, and then out of nowhere, Tommy tackled me! I can't feel my ribs!"

Boon and Foon said nothing. They were just enjoying the show.

Miss Egghead squinted her tiny eyes back and forth between Tommy and Trent. She took a deep breath and kneeled down to a confused Tommy.

"Is this true, Tommy?" she asked, placing her hand on his shoulder.

Tommy did nothing. He couldn't talk. He couldn't defend himself.

Then he had an idea.

Tommy yanked out a white rock from one of his pockets, and on one of the ripped pages from the book, he went to draw a picture for Miss Egghead.

But he couldn't.

Tommy was afraid. He could feel Trent's evil eyes watching him. Tommy slowly put the rock back into his pocket.

"Tommy," Miss Egghead said, "I'm going to send a mermaid to your mother to let her know she needs to come pick you up. I'll decide your punishment tomorrow. Tackling other kids is unacceptable."

Behind Miss Egghead, Trent, Boon, and Foon quietly laughed and pointed.

Tommy frowned and pulled his hood tightly over his head. A piece of paper landed softly on his boot. He quickly snagged it before the wind blew it away. It was a torn page from the *Book of Wizards* – the same page I-doll and himself were reading that morning.

What would a wizard have done? Tommy thought.

After lunch, Tommy was picked up from school. But he wasn't picked up by his mother.

CHAPTER THREE

THE PIZZA PIRATE

Tommy's uncle was bringing him home on an old pirate ship. At the top of the mast, a flag with a pirate hook and pizza flapped in the wind.

Tommy leaned over the edge of his uncle's ship, the mist from the ocean waves cooled his warm face. In the distance, he watched his school and the island shrink as they sailed further away.

Annoyed by the noisy seagulls that screamed and flapped above, Tommy darted to the corner of the ship and crossed his legs on the damp floor. He pulled a white rock from his pocket and began drawing on the deck – the floor of the ship.

He drew the bullies from school; Trent, Boon, and Foon. The little stick figures looked large and mean.

Tommy thought back to what had happened under his favorite tree. Trent had tricked Tommy into becoming the bad kid.

But Tommy wasn't so bad, was he? he wondered.

Tommy cringed at the awful sound of wood scraping across the deck.

It was Uncle Rick with his wooden leg wobbling towards Tommy.

With his one good eye, Uncle Rick looked down at Tommy, the other eye was covered by a purple patch.

Tommy never really looked into anyone's eyes, let alone one eye.

Uncle Rick lifted his hand to Tommy, except it wasn't a hand. Instead, his uncle had a large silver hook at the end of his arm. It had two slices of pizza hanging from its pointy end. There was always a slice of pizza on his hook.

"Pizza, Tommy?" Uncle Rick asked.

Tommy pushed his uncle's hook away.

"Yarr', me gots' myself a new name, Tommy," said Uncle Rick. "They call me *The Pizza Pirate!* Me loves it! The Pizza Pirate! It's catchy, isn't it? They say me pizza's the best in the land."

Tommy continued staring at his drawing of the bullies.

The Pizza Pirate caught a glimpse of the drawing with his one eye before Tommy wiped it away with his cloak.

"What are ye' doing, nephy'?" The Pizza Pirate asked Tommy. "Tackling kids at school like that? Yarr'! It's not like ye'."

Tommy bit his lip but jumped to his feet when a sharp whistle drew him back to the side of the ship. He leaned over and looked deep into the splashing, blue water.

There was nothing there.

Splash! A shiny mermaid jumped up and whipped the wet purple hair out of her face. She was carrying a flat, square crate that smelled of cheese.

Tommy laughed as the water from the mermaid's wet hair sprinkled all over him.

The mermaid sparkled in the sunlight like a shiny diamond, and she had a scaly tail instead of legs!

Tommy wiggled the toes in his boots, wondering what a tail instead of legs would be like. Then Tommy realized something.

Why was he still wearing his boots?

Tommy kicked his boots off and tossed them to the side.

"Hi, Tommy!" The mermaid smiled. "I haven't seen you in a while! Will you help me out and put this pizza crate over with the others?"

Tommy took the pizza crate from the mermaid and opened it up. There was no pizza in it. Just some left over melted cheese, but it still smelled good.

The Pizza Pirate placed his cold, silver hook on Tommy's shoulder. "Tommy, will ye' put the crate over by the pizza oven?" he asked. "And me hopes ye' don't mind, me needs to deliver a pizza to some friends before me drops ye' off at home."

With the empty pizza crate, Tommy scampered over to the pizza oven.

The large oven appeared to be made of stone and had a small opening in the front. Inside the gap, fire sparked, and heat poured out of it. Tommy had never seen anything like this before, let alone on a pirate ship.

"Excuse me, lad," said one of the other crewmen aboard the ship. He carried a cold pizza on a giant, flat shovel.

Tommy jumped out of the way, still holding the empty pizza crate.

The crewman placed the cold pizza in front of the heated gap of the pizza oven. It didn't take long for the cheese on the pizza to melt.

Tommy sniffed the delicious air and fell into a daydream full of endless pizza. But another sharp whistle quickly snapped Tommy awake.

Next to the pizza oven, dozens of empty pizza crates laid scattered across the deck.

Tommy set the crate he was carrying

aside and began picking up the other crates. He neatly stacked the crates into a perfectly straight tower, much like the way he stacked the books in his bedroom.

"Tommy, open up one of those crates for me, will ye'?" The Pizza Pirate asked as he pulled the pizza out of the oven with the flat shovel.

After taking the time to decide what crate to use, Tommy finally chose one and yanked the crate out from the stack. He opened up the creaky crate for his uncle.

"Yarr'! This pizza is more appetizing than some buried booty on a treasure island," said The Pizza Pirate, laughing. He slid the steaming pizza into the crate.

"Now, take that wonderful work of pizza-art to the lovely mermaid over there, please?" The Pizza Pirate asked his nephew.

Tommy nodded and sprinted to the side of the ship.

With a glowing smile, the mermaid took the pizza. "Thank you, Tommy!" she said. "I hope to see you again soon! You're such a sweet kid."

Tommy smiled and placed his hand on his chin to thank the mermaid as she splashed into the sea.

Holding the pizza crate just above the water, the mermaid flapped her sparkly tail and swam toward a tiny boat not far from them.

Crammed inside that small boat was a

family of dwarves.

The short, hairy dwarves burst with excitement as the mermaid approached.

They snatched the pizza from the mermaid, opened up the crate, and chomped down every slice within seconds. Their beards were covered with crumbs and cheese.

Tommy giggled. Even the little children dwarves had dirty beards now.

But Tommy's smile faded away.

A thick fog rolled in between them and the boat of dwarves.

Tommy could barely see a thing – even the sunlight was lost in the fog.

A moment later, the fog cleared a bit. A dark ship with purple sails approached. It must have been twice as big as The Pizza Pirate's ship.

Tommy had a bad feeling about this.

CHAPTER FOUR

CHAINS WITH TEETH

The Pizza Pirate tapped his wooden leg on the deck with excitement as the foggy ship neared closer and closer.

"Well, kiss me mama and eat a pizza!" cried The Pizza Pirate. "We've got us a big order coming up, lads!"

The Pizza Pirate took a huge bite out of the pizza slice hanging from his hook and tugged a rope hanging from above.

Tommy's eyes shot up.

Bells near the top of the sails clattered cheerfully, ringing out into the open sea.

The eager crewmen jumped to their feet.

"New customer!" they shouted and prepared some fresh pizzas to put in the pizza oven.

Crash! Tommy stumbled as the mysterious ship slammed into them.

A bridge creeped out from the foggy ship and dropped at Tommy's bare feet.

The deck was so foggy now, Tommy couldn't see his uncle, the other crewmen, or even the pizza oven.

Tommy shivered as a clanging sound slithered between his legs. He looked down, and wrapped around his feet were black chains.

More chains dangled out from the fog and rattled in Tommy's face.

Tommy's eyes shot forward.

Inches away from his nose, a chain with a metal head and sharp teeth hissed at Tommy like a snake.

"Easy there, Snakey-Chains," a voice echoed from the foggy ship. "Don't bite the boy's face off just yet."

A robed man with a big pointy hat glided across the bridge and stopped in front of Tommy and the hissing chains. He carried a long staff in his skinny hands. At the end of the staff was a ring with teeth all around the inside of it – almost like something small was supposed to go into the ring.

Tommy squinted. The robed man looked familiar to him. He reached into his pocket and took out the only page left from *The*

Book of Wizards.

Tommy looked closely. The wizard in the drawing had a pointy hat, a long beard, and a staff.

He stared at the man again. This man had a pointy hat, a long beard, and a staff as well.

A wizard. How did he not know this? Tommy thought. He had only read it a hundred times with I-doll.

The wizard spoke to the chains with teeth that slithered around Tommy. "That's enough," he said. "Snakey-Chains, back away from the boy."

Tommy let out a deep breath as the snapping Snakey-Chain slithered away from his face.

"Remarkable, aren't they?" the wizard asked Tommy. "My Snakey-Chains? I found them tangled up and stuck under some rocks deep in a cave. I freed them."

A couple of the Snakey-Chains gently slithered up and rested their metal heads on the wizard's shoulders.

"The Snakey-Chains serve me now," the wizard said. "They're perfect."

Tommy bit his lip. The slithering chains with teeth did not come off as kind or gentle. But the staff the wizard was holding, that seemed interesting.

Tommy reached his hand out. The tips of his fingers barely grazed the staff. The rough wood reminded him of I-doll.

"Oh, easy there, Tommy," the wizard

said as he yanked his staff away. "A wizard's staff is not a toy. The name's Wiz, by the way. Wiz the Wizard." As Wiz introduced himself to Tommy, his busy eyes searched all around.

"Where's the other one?" Wiz asked, quickly tapping his foot.

Tommy looked all around himself, but he wasn't sure who Wiz was talking about. *His brother? I-doll? Uncle Rick?*

"Ahoy! What in mother's muffins is going on here?" The Pizza Pirate shouted. He burst through the fog carrying a tall stack of ready-to-go pizzas. "A wizard! What ye' doing on me ship? We don't do no dining on me ship! It's take-out only!"

"Ah, you must be the famous Pizza Pirate?" the wizard asked. He waved his staff above his head, and more Snakey-Chains slithered aboard the ship, hissing and snapping.

Grinning ear to ear, The Pizza Pirate jumped with excitement. "I'm famous?" he asked cheerfully. "Well, shiver me timbers! It's about time!"

The Pizza Pirate dropped the pizzas on the deck, drew his sword, and pointed it at Wiz the Wizard.

"I'm still going to need ye' to get off me ship, ye' warp-headed wizard!"

Wiz chuckled. "Your Uncle is quite amusing," said Wiz as he turned his attention back to Tommy. "Well, since the whole family isn't here, you and I will be

24

leaving then, Tommy."

"Avast, wizard! Ye' ain't taking the boy anywhere!" The Pizza Pirate lunged at Wiz with the point of his sword.

But a Snakey-Chain hissed angrily. It wrapped around The Pizza Pirate's sword and snapped it right in half.

The Pizza Pirate stumbled and fell on his bum.

Another Snakey-Chain wrapped up Tommy like a snake would with its prey.

Fighting to breathe, Tommy stretched and squirmed. He was nearly free. But two more Snakey-Chains zipped around Tommy. Tommy wasn't getting out now.

"You're pretty strong for your age, Tommy," Wiz said.

But Tommy wasn't listening. Tommy was so out of breath from the squeezing of the Snakey-Chains, he laid his head back and passed out.

"Time to go," Wiz told his Snakey-Chains.

"Wizard!" The Pizza Pirate shouted as he picked up the pizzas. "Let's cut a deal. Take the pizzas. Free! On the house! Just leave me nephew."

Wiz laughed. "How about I take both?" he said. "Tommy and I might be out at The Sea of Dragons for a while."

Wiz waved his staff, and the Snakey-Chains dragged a sleeping Tommy aboard the wizard's ship.

Another Snakey-Chain snatched the

pizzas from The Pizza Pirate and slithered across the ramp.

Wiz followed.

Two more Snakey-Chains slithered around the mast of The Pizza Pirate's ship and snapped it in half. The sails came crashing down.

"No! Me ship! Ye' won't get away with this!" The Pizza Pirate yelled at Wiz. "Chris and I-doll, they'll come looking for Tommy."

Wiz turned and smiled. "I'm counting on it."

CHAPTER FIVE

A MERMAID WITH A MESSAGE

With each step, his armor clicked and clanged as Chris journeyed deeper into the mountain. The fiery torch in his hand flickered in his blue eyes.

Chris froze as a deep growl echoed through the dark caves. He slowly drew his sword.

"Here, dragon, dragon, dragon - where are you?" Chris called out.

Roar!

The cave shook.

Rocks and rubble rained down from

above.

"Finally." Chris smiled.

The dragon attacked from above.

Chris leapt like a frog and rolled out of the way of the dragon's fiery breath.

"Gotta' be quicker than that, dragon!" Chris shouted.

The stomping dragon turned and lunged at Chris with its chomping teeth.

"For a dragon, your breath smells surprisingly nice."

Chris jumped high into the air and over the dragon. With one quick slice of his sword, he chopped the dragon's tail clean off.

The dragon laid there, moaning in pain.

Chris hovered above the dragon's head with his sword held high. He was just about to slay the scaly beast when the dragon looked at him.

"Wake up," said the dragon.

"Huh?" Chris asked, his face scrunched up.

"Boy, I said wake up!"

Chris shot up from his nap! As he laid there on the swaying dock, the smell of salt water and seaweed tickled his nostrils.

"Wake up, boy!" I-doll smacked Chris on the head with his tiny wooden hand.

"Ouch, alright, I'm awake! Stop hitting me!" Chris yelled at I-doll. He covered his eyes from the blinding sun and gazed out to the open sea – not a ship or boat anywhere – just splashing blue waves.

"We've only been at the docks for five minutes, and you fell asleep, boy!" I-doll yelled at Chris, his tiny legs pacing back and forth down the dock. "Tommy will be here any minute! And I haven't seen him all day!"

"You saw him this morning," said Chris. "Remember? When we broke the breakfast table? Did you help mother fix it?"

"Bah! Boy, that was forever ago!" I-doll cried. "And no, no your mother moved her 'thing' to the armory."

Chris moved on from the broken breakfast table to his brother. "What do you think happened?" Chris asked I-doll, scratching his chin. "Do you think Tommy attacked another kid on purpose?"

I-doll scratched his pointy head. "Hmm, boy, it's not like him. Tommy's always played rough, but he's never attacked anybody for no reason."

"There's something fishy going on," said Chris, "and it stinks... like fish."

"Boy, I don't like it. Tommy could get kicked out of school!" I-doll shouted. "Speaking of schools, why aren't you in school right now, boy?"

"It's kind of a funny story. Billy snuck a dragon egg into school," Chris said, laughing. "During lunch, the egg hatched and burnt down half the school."

"You're right, boy. That is funny," I-doll joked. "A foolish kid caused a school to burn down."

"Just part of the school burnt down," Chris explained.

"Alright, boy. Never mind," I-doll said, changing the subject. "What were you dreaming about? You were kicking in your sleep."

"I was about to slay a dragon," Chris said. "Then you smacked me in the head. I think you gave me a splinter." Chris rubbed his head, picking through his golden forest of hair.

I-doll shrugged. "It's not my fault your father carved me out of wood. And I thought you liked dragons?"

"When they're not trying to eat me," Chris said. "Most of them try to eat me." He looked around the docks for his helmet. It should have been laying there next to him. "Where the dragons is my helmet?"

A second later, Chris noticed two seagulls fighting over his helmet, tugging at it with their orange beaks.

"Hey!" Chris screamed at the seagulls, running and waving his arms. "You annoying birds, drop it!"

The seagulls dropped the helmet and flapped away. It almost sounded like they were laughing at Chris.

"I'm tired of these seagulls," Chris cried. "They're everywhere all of a sudden – screaming and pooping everywhere." He picked up his helmet and tried to clean it with his blue cape. "Going to have to have mother re-shine my helmet again. This is why I don't like taking it off."

"Boy, one of these days, a seagull's going to carry me away," I-doll told Chris. He looked out to the sea for Tommy and The Pizza Pirate. "His school's not that far. Where's Tommy?"

Splash! A sparkling mermaid popped out of the water next to Chris and I-doll.

"Chris! I-doll! It's Tommy!" the mermaid yelled. "A wizard's taken him into The Sea of Dragons!"

CHAPTER SIX

THE ROUND KING

With I-doll on his shoulder, Chris rushed to his mother. The king's castle towered beyond their tiny village as he came up to an old barn. A sign reading 'Armory' hung above the entrance.

Chris and I-doll burst through the doors. Inside, a handful of women smacked heated rods of iron with oversized hammers.

Cling! Clang! The blaring sound stung Chris to his spine.

"Boy, that's so loud!" I-doll cried. He tried to muffle the sound with Chris's cape.

Mother stood up in front of the ladies, showing the women how to make, or forge, new swords.

Cling! Clang!

"Alright, ladies, don't stop!" mother yelled over the loud hammering. "Flatten out the rod. Make the edges sharp and straight. It's not about strength. It's all about skill."

Cling! Clang!

Chris smacked his forehead. "Oh, dragon farts," he cried. "Mother's having a sword-making class again."

Cling! Clang!

"What?" I-doll yelled. He couldn't hear Chris over the loud hammering.

Cling! Clang!

Chris shouted back, "I said, mother's having another sword-making class!"

Cling! Clang!

I-doll threw his arms up in the air. "I can't hear you!" he shouted back. "Your mother's sword-making class is too loud!"

Chris shook his head. He rushed up front, waving his arms, and tried to get his mother's attention.

"Mother!"

Mother looked up with a big smile and sweat running down her face. "Hi, sweetie! It will just be a little bit longer!"

"Mother, Tommy's been taken!"

Mother's smile quickly disappeared. She dropped her hammer and the sword she was making. The other women did as well.

"Oh, finally," I-doll cried. "That hammering sound was giving me a splitting headache."

"What! What do you mean?" mother asked Chris as she wiped the sweat and black stuff from her face.

"We were waiting for Uncle Rick to drop off Tommy at the docks, and they never showed up," Chris explained. "One of Uncle Rick's pizza mermaids showed up and said a wizard with magic chains took Tommy to the Sea of Dragons!"

Chris's stomach suddenly growled loudly through the quiet barn.

I-doll tapped on Chris's head. "Really, boy? You're still hungry at a time like this?"

"My stomach doesn't know what time it is. It wants pizza. It's pizza time."

Mother shook her long face and turned to the women in the barn. "Ladies, we'll have to finish our swords another day. I'm sorry."

The ladies turned and quietly left the barn.

"We must get to the king," mother told her son and I-doll. "We're going to need a boat."

I-doll grumbled, "Oh, boy. We will be lucky if the king lifts a pinky for us."

●●●

Inside the castle, the grumpy king spat out at Chris, I-doll, and mother. He sat there, squeezed into his tiny throne.

"The Sea of Dragons!" the king yelled.

Crumbs flew out of king's mouth with a half-eaten pizza next to him. With a deep breath, he shoved a whole slice of pizza into his mouth.

The king shouted some more. "You're crazier than a witch riding a donkey if you think I'm going to give you a boat."

"My lord, please?" mother cried. "Any ship will work. That's my baby boy out there."

Atop Chris's shoulder, I-doll whispered into the boy's ear, "Look how big the king's getting? He's so large. He just keeps eating."

"Be quiet, I-doll," Chris snapped, shaking his shoulder.

"I won't waste a ship by sending it into The Sea of Dragons!" shouted the king, his awful voice echoed through the castle. "I might as well set the ship on fire!" He pounded his fist. "And, I heard from a little birdy, your 'baby boy', Tommy, tackled another kid at school."

Chris, I-doll, and mother glanced at each other with disappointing eyes.

"My lord, we don't know the whole story yet," mother pleaded. "We may never know the whole story if we can't get Tommy back."

"There's no excuse for fighting at school!" The king shouted, slamming his fist on the throne.

From the shadows, a princess in a bright red dress softly stepped next to the king.

"Father, what have I told you about your temper?" The princess warned the king. "And that's enough pizza for you. It's going to kill you."

The princess took the rest of the pizzas away from the angry king.

"Wha- What! Grr... Fine," the king grumbled, crossing his arms over his chest.

Chris stared at the princess with half a smile.

The princess brushed the soft hair out of her eyes and smiled back. The purple flowers wrapped around her head really brought life to the dull throne room.

"Hey, boy, she's kind of cute," I-doll whispered as he tapped on Chris's head. "I bet she'd go dragon slaying with you."

Chris shook his shoulder again, his face turning bright red. "Quiet, I-doll. We don't have time for this."

Chris lifted his shoulders and stomped his foot at the stubborn king. "My brother needs us!" Chris yelled. "Now, are you going to help us or not?"

The king huffed and puffed as he popped himself out of his throne. He glared at Chris with his droopy eyes.

"Never," the king said, stomping his oversized foot down. "You will need a miracle to save Tommy!"

Chris looked to the princess for help.

But the princess frowned and turned away.

CHAPTER SEVEN

DO YOU LIKE PINEAPPLE PIZZA?

"What a waste of time!" Chris yelled as he kicked open the tall doors leading out of the castle.

Mother followed behind, crying in her hands.

"That king is nothing but a worthless, troll butt sniffing, piece of garbage!" I-doll yelled, waving his little fist at the castle. "And after all we did for him and his kingdom! I don't get it. How is that man still a king?"

"His grandfather was a king," Chris

explained. "Then his father was a king. And now he is a king. It's in his blood."

"His blood's probably mostly cheese and pizza sauce by now," I-doll joked. "Did you see how big he's gotten? I bet he could feed a family of dragons for an entire year!"

"I doubt even dragons would eat him," said Chris. "He's so rotten inside."

"True... very true." I-doll nodded.

Outside of the castle stood their small village. Not many lived here, but it was always loud and busy. The farms to the west grew their fruits and vegetables. And past the stone houses to the east, the docks stretched out into the open sea.

Chris scratched his chin, gazing past the docks at the cloudy sea. "Who else has a boat that we could use?" Chris asked. "Somebody has to have one."

"Oh, my little Tommy," mother cried. "Stuck in The Sea of Dragons! I will find someone to help us!"

Mother panicked and ran through the village, begging for help. At one point, a knight on horseback nearly trampled mother as she jumped in front of him.

"The Sea of Dragons? You're crazy, lady!" the knight yelled at mother before riding away.

Chris and I-doll watched mother jump in and out of houses and farms. One man chased her off with a broom. Another, threw a couple of clucking chickens at her.

"My mother's crazy," Chris said, shaking his head.

"Yeah, boy. It must run in the family," I-doll joked.

"Christopher?" a soft voice whispered from behind.

"Dragon farts!" Chris yelled, startled by the quiet princess. "Princess, where'd you come from?"

"Girl, you scared the splinters out of me!" I-doll cried.

"Oh, forgive me. It's my quiet feet."

Chris straightened out his armor and wiped the dirt from his pants. He couldn't do much about the rips and holes in his cape. "Something we can do for you, princess?" Chris asked.

"I would like to help."

"Help? How can you help us?" I-doll asked, shaking his tiny fist at her. "Your dad wouldn't lift a finger for us."

"I know, but you saved my father's life before, and I want to help you," the princess said as she held up a rolled piece of paper to Chris.

"What's this?" Chris asked, taking the note from her warm hands.

"Take that note to the docks," she answered. "The sea captain there, he will give you a ship."

Chris and I-doll squinted at each other with curious eyes.

"How can we trust you?" Chris asked.

"Well, I – uh – just want to help, like I said."

I-doll jumped with an idea. "Princess, I have a question for you," said I-doll. "Do you like pineapple on your pizza?"

The princess looked deep in thought. "I don't believe I've ever tried pizza with pineapple on it," she said. "But it sounds good."

"It's disgusting!" Chris shouted.

"Princess, only the worst people in the world like pineapple pizza!" yelled I-doll.

The princess giggled. "Well, I'll have to try it and let you know," said the princess. "Now please, trust me. Take the letter and get a boat. Find your brother."

Chris nodded and put the letter in his pocket.

"Very well, it's our only option," said Chris. He turned to I-doll. "Alright, let's get my mother before she gets ran over by a horse."

I-doll looked for mother. "Boy, I don't see her. I think maybe the chickens got her." I-doll laughed. "Ha! Death by chickens! I'm just kidding, but I really don't see her."

"You'd better go find her," the princess told Chris. "And then, go find your brother."

"Thank you, princess," Chris said. He turned and ran through the village.

"You're welcome! Good luck!" The princess waved.

41

"Boy, I think I like her," I-doll told Chris.

Chris's face turned bright red again. He shook his head and snapped at I-doll, "We don't have time for princesses, I-doll. We've got to find Tommy and find out what this wizard wants."

CHAPTER EIGHT

THE WIZARD

Aboard the wizard's foggy ship, Tommy woke up face down on the deck. The damp wood felt nice and cool on his warm cheek.

Two little feet scampered next to Tommy.

Tommy thought it was I-doll, but it turned out to be an annoying seagull, squawking and chirping.

Tommy slowly pushed himself up and waved the seagull away. He rubbed his head, trying to remember what happened.

Where was he? Oh, that's right. A wizard named 'Wiz' had taken him from his uncle. But why?

With all of the fog swaying across the deck, it was a little hard to see around the wizard's ship. There was no sign of the Snakey-Chains or Wiz.

A faint orange glow peeked through the fog from what looked to be the back of the ship.

Tommy slowly tiptoed toward it.

He came to a small fire. Hanging above the fire was a large black bowl with a greenish goo boiling inside. Next to it laid a bunch of crates and bottles.

And the pizza!

The pizza crates were scattered all over the deck, like someone had just thrown them there.

Tommy hopped over and neatly stacked the pizza crates on top of each other as they should have been. Once he was happy with the stacking, Tommy threw open the top crate and yanked out a slice of pizza.

Biting into the pizza, Tommy smiled. The pizza was not frozen or warm. It was just a little cold… It was perfect.

Tommy sat next to the warm fire with the whole slice of pizza in his mouth. He took out the white rock from his pocket and started drawing on the deck.

The white rock scraped across the wood as Tommy drew his favorite tree, the bullies from school, and the torn in half book. And below all of it, he drew a sad

Tommy.

Maybe the bullies were right. Tommy had thought. *Maybe he was a dummy. After all, he fell for Trent's shady trick that got him sent home.*

Then Tommy remembered, he hadn't made it home yet.

"Those are some mean looking kids you've drawn, Tommy," Wiz spoke, hovering behind.

Tommy jumped and chuckled nervously.

"I see. The puzzle pieces are coming together," said Wiz. "I was wondering why your uncle picked you up from school early." Wiz smiled, tilting his pointy hat up.

Tommy stood up and peered over the side of the boat. He couldn't see anything through the thick fog, but Tommy thought about jumping over and swimming away.

"Those kids were making fun of you, weren't they, Tommy?" Wiz asked. "Maybe they destroyed something you liked?"

Tommy dragged his hand across the ledge of the ship. The rough wood reminded him of I-doll. I-doll would get mad if Tommy jumped, but I-doll wasn't here, so he went to lift one leg over the side.

Wiz creeped closer to Tommy. "Maybe we can help each other, Tommy," said Wiz.

Tommy put his leg down.

"I know what it's like to be different,"

Wiz told Tommy. "Many won't understand you. So, they'll make fun of you. You'll make a lot of enemies, but I can show you how to be stronger than them."

Tommy made his way back to the small fire and stared into the flames.

"Tommy, you don't speak," said Wiz. "So, the only way to express yourself is through actions. I like you, Tommy. And I want to show you one of the great powers in the land."

Tommy watched curiously as Wiz waved his staff in the air with excitement.

"Magic, Tommy. Magic that can raise mountains! Magic that can lift walls of water in the sea! Magic that can bring flames to a sword!"

Tommy was curious. All of this talk of magic sounded incredible… and powerful.

Wiz waved his staff around again. "I'm talking about the magic of Dragon Stones!" he shouted.

Tommy scratched his head. *Dragon Stones?* Tommy called back to earlier that morning when I-doll was reading *The Book of Wizards* to him. That's right, wizards get their magic from Dragon Stones.

But where did the Dragon Stones come from? Tommy wondered.

"I'm going to show you what Dragon Stones can do." Wiz smiled down at Tommy. "But first, we are going to need a dragon," he said, waving his staff in the air once again.

A second later, two Snakey-Chains slithered between Tommy and Wiz, carrying a crate of pizza.

Wiz opened the crate. "Not many know this," he said. "But most dragons love cold pizza. It's the perfect bait."

Wiz waved his staff again.

The Snakey-Chains each grabbed a slice of pizza with their sharp teeth and slithered over the side of the ship. They hung out there like they were fishing.

But Wiz wasn't trying to catch some fish.

CHAPTER NINE

SICK DRAGONS

A few moments had passed. Tommy didn't blink once before he heard the cries and screeches of a trapped dragon splashing down below.

The Snakey-Chains began reeling in the catch.

Wiz smiled at Tommy. "That didn't take long at all," he said.

Tommy bit his lip. The crying from the dragon grew louder and louder. He wasn't too fond of dragons, but this just didn't feel right to him.

The Snakey-Chains finished pulling in

the wet dragon and pinned it to the deck.

This dragon had green, slimy scales and large, flappy ears. After a bit more struggling, the dragon gave up and laid its cold head at Tommy's bare feet.

"Looks like we caught us a Sea Dragon," Wiz said frowning. "It's a young one, though. It'll have to do."

Tommy jumped back from the slimy Sea Dragon.

Wiz set his staff down next to the steaming, black bowl.

"This large bowl is a cauldron, Tommy," said Wiz. "I use it to make potions... and sometimes soup."

The wizard shuffled through a bunch of crates and bottles before he pulled out an old book. He threw it open and quickly flipped through the pages.

"Ah, here we are," said Wiz, pointing in the book. "We need a giant's toenail." Wiz took out a giant's toenail from a crate and handed it to Tommy.

Tommy held the heavy giant's toenail in his hands. It smelled old and rotten, and it kind of felt like wood.

"Toss it in, Tommy," said Wiz.

Tommy tossed the giant's toenail into the boiling cauldron.

Wiz pointed to the book again. "Next, we need the hair of a troll." Wiz handed Tommy a handful of troll hair.

Tommy tossed it in.

"And finally, we need three goblin

eyeballs." Wiz handed Tommy three goblin eyeballs.

Tommy chuckled nervously as the slimy eyeballs looked at him, but he quickly threw them into the cauldron.

Tommy covered his nose and leaned away from the boiling goo inside the cauldron. It smelled worse than his brother's feet after knight training.

"Hand me that bowl sitting on that crate there, will you?" Wiz asked Tommy.

Tommy grabbed the empty bowl and handed it to Wiz.

Wiz dipped the bowl into the cauldron and filled it with the stinky, gross soup. With an evil glare, Wiz turned to the Sea Dragon.

"Watch now, Tommy," said Wiz as he leaned down to the dragon.

The Snakey-Chains slithered over and forced open the dragon's mouth.

The dragon cried a little but was too tired to fight it.

Wiz carefully poured the smelly soup down the dragon's throat.

The dragon let out a little belch and shivered away the bad taste. The scaly beast laid its head back down as the Snakey-Chains let go.

Tommy shrugged.

Nothing was happening.

It just seemed like Wiz fed the dragon some smelly soup.

But then the Sea Dragon turned pale,

and its eyes stopped glowing.

It looked sick.

The Sea Dragon opened its mouth and coughed. And then a deep cough. *Cough! Cough!* The dragon was coughing like it was choking on something.

"Perfect." Wiz smiled. "Dragons almost never get sick, Tommy. But the younger the dragon, the easier it is to make them sick."

Tommy watched the helpless Sea Dragon cough and cough. *Why would anyone want to make a dragon sick?* he thought.

And with one last cough, the dragon spat out a bunch of stones.

Two of the stones were blue and glowing.

Dragon Stones!

One of the Dragon Stones bounced over by Tommy's foot.

Tommy looked at Wiz.

Wiz didn't see the second Dragon Stone by Tommy's foot.

Tommy quickly put his toes over it. The Dragon Stone felt a little wet and chilly.

Wiz leaned down and picked up the other Dragon Stone by the Sea Dragon's nose.

"But, when dragon's do get sick, they make these," Wiz said. "These are Dragon Stones. The *real* magic."

"Sea Dragons cough up Water Stones. Fire Dragons cough up Fire Stones. Ice

Dragons cough up Ice Stones and so on."

Wiz took a deep breath and closed his eyes. "There's another Dragon Stone," Wiz said. He seemed amazed to be talking about it. "An Earth Stone. They come from Earth Dragons. They're very rare, and sometimes, they have the power to bring life to things that aren't."

Wiz paced around.

"And there's so much more I don't know about the Earth Stone!" Wiz cried, rubbing his beard. "But, we will find out together, Tommy."

Tommy pondered. *The wizard, the staff, the Dragon Stones, all of it was just like it said in The Book of Wizards.*

Then Tommy noticed Wiz's staff laying there against the stack of pizza crates.

Grinning ear to ear, Wiz stared at the sparkling, blue Water Stone.

"This Water Stone is far from rare," Wiz said. He put the stone inside his pocket. "But it still might be useful."

Tommy leapt and grabbed Wiz's staff!

Startled, Wiz spun around. "Tommy! No!" he yelled.

Just like Wiz was doing before, Tommy waved the staff in the air. He tried to draw the Snakey-Chains away from the Sea Dragon.

Tommy's plan had worked.

The Snakey-Chains slithered away and chased after Tommy.

Wiz grabbed Tommy's arm and tried to

take back his staff.

But Tommy was strong. Like a boulder, he didn't budge – not yet.

"Let go of it, Tommy!" Wiz shouted, pulling with all of his might.

The Snakey-Chains slithered around Tommy's legs and tied his arms up to his chest.

Wiz easily took back his staff.

Tommy peeked behind Wiz to see the Sea Dragon wiggle over the side of the ship and leap into the sea.

Tommy smiled.

Wiz spun around to see the Sea Dragon was gone and heard the faint sounds of splashes over the side. He turned and glared down at Tommy.

"You're clever, Tommy," Wiz said. "But that Sea Dragon may have been useful."

Tommy could barely breathe from the squeezing of the Snakey-Chains. His eyes became very heavy and closed shut.

"You're lucky I like you," Wiz spoke to a passed-out Tommy. "I should throw you overboard for that."

CHAPTER TEN

A COOL SWORD

"I've got pizzas!" I-doll shouted, holding crates of pizzas over his head. He scampered across the bobbing sea dock over to Chris.

Chris scratched his head, examining the so-called boat rocking in the ocean waves. He held up a small, empty bucket.

I-doll stopped next to him and set the pizzas on the dock. He took a long look at the boat with Chris. "What a piece of junk!" I-doll yelled. "It's so tiny. Is it leaking? There's water in the bottom of it."

Chris frowned and held up the tiny bucket. "Yes," he said. "The captain said to use this bucket here to empty out the water every few hours, and we'll be fine." Chris shrugged.

"I think we'd be better off swimming to The Sea of Dragons," I-doll joked.

"It's going to have to do," said Chris. "There's no other boats here."

Chris could now smell the tasty pizzas over the salty sea water. "Good thinking, I-doll," Chris said, rubbing his stomach. "I'm going to need something to eat on the way there. And the way back."

Chris hopped into their tiny boat and started to open up the sail, but then decided he'd better empty the water from the bottom of the boat first.

I-doll leaned against the pizza crates on the dock. "Yeah, boy, I snuck back into the castle and took them from the king," he said." I'm doing the king a favor, really. He doesn't need more pizzas … But they're not for you, boy. They're for the Sea Dragons."

"What? The Sea Dragons? What are you talking about?" Chris asked, his stomach growling.

"Boy, everyone knows Sea Dragons love pizza," I-doll explained. "If you bump into some Sea Dragons, offer them a slice of pizza, and maybe they won't eat you."

"Not your worst idea," said Chris, nodding in agreement. "Alright, grab the pizzas and hop in."

I-doll froze. "Wha-what? I'm not going. You know how I feel about water," he cried. "I can't get wet. I'll swell up!"

"You'll be fine. Just – hang on tight."

"That's your plan – hang on tight?"

"Tommy needs you. You understand him better than most," Chris explained to I-doll. "And I don't want this wizard teaching Tommy any bad habits. Mother wants good examples for him."

"Yeah, boy. You're right. Of course, I'm going," I-doll said. "But you might want to stop with the burping contests at the breakfast table, if you want to be a good example."

Chris laughed. "We all know I won that contest," Chris said proudly.

"Not something to be proud of," said I-doll as he jumped into the tiny boat, carrying the pizzas over his head.

"Christopher! Wait!" mother shouted as she ran across the dock through a group of seagulls. She held a long, wrapped object in her arms.

Chris scratched his chin, wondering how mother was going to fit in the tiny boat with them.

"Hello, mother," said Chris. "This boat is very small. I'm not sure if we'll all fit in here."

"It's fine, sweetie. You know I don't know how to use a sword." Mother shrugged. "I would just get in the way."

Then her face lit up with excitement.

"But I know how to make swords!" mother yelled. "Look!"

Mother laid down the wrapped objects she was carrying and opened them up on the deck. Inside was a shiny sword and shield. Both of them were glowing with an icy-blue color.

Chris's jaw dropped to the bottom of the leaking boat. His eyes popped out of his face.

"Are those for me?" Chris screeched.

"I just finished making these," mother said. "The sword is for you, and the shield is for Tommy."

Chris picked up the shiny, new sword and examined it from top to bottom. "Wow. It's so... so cool," he said. "It's kind of cold, like ice. It's cool."

I-doll giggled. "Ha! It's *literally* cool."

"Yes," mother said. "I traded a couple of pizzas to some fishermen for some... uh... Dragon Stones."

Chris looked at mother with curious eyes.

"I think they're Ice Stones," mother said. "Anyway, your sword has an Ice Stone at the bottom of the hilt, and Tommy's shield has one on the front. They came out perfect. They should easily cut through anything that's hot – like Fire Dragons, Desert Demons, Lava Monsters..."

"Or pizza!" I-doll laughed.

Chris paused, scratching his chin again.

"Wait a minute, Dragon Stones?" Chris asked mother. "I thought you said Dragon Stones were dangerous and should never be played with."

Mother put her hands on her hips and glared down at Chris. "First of all, I didn't *play* with them," she snapped. "And second, I trust you boys to use these weapons for good... even though you boys broke my table this morning."

Chris kind of looked away, pretending not to hear that last part.

"Well, thank you, mother," said Chris. "This sword is really cool. I can't wait to try it out."

"Boy, Chris," I-doll said, hopping up on Chris's shoulder, "if you keep staring at that sword like that, the princess might get jealous."

"The princess isn't here!" Chris snapped. "I mean... be quiet, I-doll! No time for princesses."

I-doll laughed. "Your face is all red!" he said. He then turned to mother. "Mommy, do you have anything for me?"

"You know what, I-doll?" mother said. "I do." She grabbed I-doll and gave him a giant hug. "Here's a giant hug for you to give to Tommy when you find him."

I-doll popped his head out of her arms.

"Gee, thanks, I guess," I-doll told mother. "I get a hug that's not even meant for me."

"Alright, I-doll, it's time to go. The sun's going to set soon," said Chris. "Hold on tight."

Chris untied the tiny boat from the dock, and they began drifting out to sea.

"Be safe! Be smart! Be brave!" mother shouted and waved. "And try to be home by supper time!"

Chris and I-doll waved from their leaky boat as they sailed to The Sea of Dragons.

●●●

Some time had passed. The orange sun started to rest on the open sea, and I-doll was... bored.

"Boy, are we there yet?" I-doll asked.

"No," said Chris.

"How about now?"

"No."

"Now?"

"No! I'll let you know," said Chris.

I-doll jumped onto Chris's shoulder and peeked through the small gap in his helmet.

"How about now?" I-doll yelled.

"I-doll!" Chris snapped. "I'm going to throw you into the water and the Sea Dragons are going to use you as a toothpick!"

"Boy, I'm just yanking your dragon tail," I-doll told Chris laughing.

But Chris didn't laugh. He noticed the

sea water changing colors. The splashing waves went from a dark blue to a slimy green.

"I-doll, look," Chris said, pointing to the water. "The water, it's changing colors. I think we're close."

Chris quickly grabbed the side of the boat as something bumped beneath them. *Bump! Bump!*

"Oh, boy." I-doll trembled. "I think we're going to need a bigger boat."

CHAPTER ELEVEN

THE SEA OF DRAGONS

Holding on for dear life, Chris and I-doll screamed as their tiny boat bounced around in the splashing waves. The pizza crates nearly toppled out of the boat.

"Not the pizzas!" I-doll shouted.

Chris slammed his foot down onto the pizzas to keep them steady.

"Hold on, I-doll!" Chris yelled.

I-doll held on tightly to Chris's cape.

"Bah! Don't let me fall into the water!" I-doll screamed.

But Chris's cape ripped!

"Boy! Help!" I-doll cried.

I-doll nearly fell into the ocean, but Chris caught him by his tiny, wooden foot just in time.

"I got ya'!" Chris yelled.

As Chris held onto I-doll with one hand, he grasped the sail with the other – all while keeping his foot down on the pizzas.

A giant, green beast rose out of the sea.

"Sea Dragon!" Chris shouted as the splashing waves began to settle down. With I-doll on his shoulder, Chris yanked out his cool sword.

"Boy, what are you doing?" I-doll whispered. "You're going to scare the Sea Dragon with your sword. It might be friendly."

"Uh, I-doll, look at its angry, yellow eyes and sharp teeth!" Chris said, pointing at the beast. "It looks hungry. It's going to eat us!"

Chris and I-doll gazed up at the towering Sea Dragon, the orange sun glowing behind. But to their surprise, the Sea Dragon yawned loudly into the sky.

"Hey! What's going on here?" the Sea Dragon spoke with a funny accent. "Who's-a-bumpin' their boat into my sea?"

Chris aimed his sword at the Sea Dragon.

The Sea Dragon leaned down and got a good look at Chris and I-doll with its large, yellow eye.

"Get back, you slimy beast!" Chris

shouted. "Or I'll send you crying to your mother!"

"Whoa! Whoa! Whoa! Are you talking to me?" the Sea Dragon asked. "Are you talking to me? You've got a lot of nerve, kid – coming into my sea, waving a sword at me."

I-doll thought it might be best to jump in. "Hello there, mister Sea Dragon, sir," he said with a shaky voice. "I'm I-doll, and this is my dim-witted friend."

"Dim-witted?" Chris asked, glaring at I-doll.

"We're very sorry," I-doll told the Sea Dragon. "We didn't mean to rush in here waving swords and stuff."

"Come on, I-doll. I've got this," Chris said. He pointed his cool sword higher.

"No, boy. You don't," I-doll snapped, smacking Chris with his tiny hand.

"Ouch! Come on!" Chris cried.

"So, you a dimwit, kid?" the Sea Dragon asked Chris.

Chris glared at I-doll, but then took a deep breath and decided to lower his sword.

"No... No, I'm not a dimwit," Chris said. "My name's Chris. I'm looking for my brother, Tommy. He was taken by a wizard. The wizard sailed this way in a dark, foggy ship."

"Well, kid, I'm Joey," said the Sea Dragon, stretching tall and proud. "And this is *my* sea. Ain't nobody coming into *my* sea without permission."

Chris and I-doll gave each other a concerned look.

"Joey the Sea Dragon," said I-doll, clearing his throat, "perhaps... maybe, we could look around anyway?"

"My brother might not fully know the danger he's in. We have to find him," Chris told the Sea Dragon.

"Yeah, I could let you in." Joey the Sea Dragon smiled. "But you gotta' give me something in return. See, that's how it works out here."

Suddenly, another Sea Dragon popped out of the water!

"What's going on here?" the other Sea Dragon asked. "Joey, are you bothering fishermen again?"

Joey the Sea Dragon rolled his eyes. "Patty? What are you doing? I thought you were taking a nap at the bottom of the sea?" asked Joey the Sea Dragon.

Patty the Sea Dragon shouted, "I was! Till I heard a bunch of yelling!"

"I'm sorry, Patty," said Joey the Sea Dragon. "This kid and his toothpick here are looking for a wizard and a brother or something... And I told them they ain't coming into *my* sea!"

"First of all," Patty the Sea Dragon snapped, "this ain't just *your* sea. And second, a ship came through here earlier. The one I told you about, with the snapping chains – the Snakey-Chains, I think they're called. I couldn't get close enough to it."

"I don't remember you saying that, Patty," said Joey the Sea Dragon.

Patty the Sea Dragon rolled her giant, yellow eyes. "Of course, you don't – because you weren't listening!"

Chris and I-doll rolled their eyes as the Sea Dragons bickered back and forth for what seemed like forever.

"Stinky dragon farts, we're never going to find Tommy," Chris cried.

"Now, you let this kid and his tooth-pick through, so they can find his brother," Patty the Sea Dragon yelled at Joey the Sea Dragon.

I-doll scratched his pointy head. "Wait, am I the toothpick?" he asked.

Chris laughed. "Yes," he said.

Joey the Sea Dragon gave up. "Fine. You can enter my – I mean, *our* sea," he said with a long face.

Chris felt a little bad for the Sea Dragon, but he had an idea.

"We have something to offer you. Sort of a thank you, I guess," Chris said to Joey the Sea Dragon. He picked up the pizza crates and held them above his head.

"Pizzas!" Chris shouted.

The two Sea Dragons drooled all over Chris and I-doll.

"Why didn't you say something earlier?" asked Joey the Sea Dragon. "I've been starving for a pizza since the Great Dragon

Wars!"

"Joey, hold onto the pizzas. I'm going to get the other Joeys," yelled Patty the Sea Dragon.

"Wait a minute, there's other Sea Dragons named 'Joey'?" I-doll asked.

"Oh, yes," said Joey the Sea Dragon as he used his slimy tail to take the pizzas from Chris. "There's Uncle Joey, Brother Joey, Cousin Joey, Father Joey, Baby Joey. All the male Sea Dragons in our family are named Joey."

"How original," I-doll joked.

Chris rolled his eyes again. "Well, we should get going," he said. "It'll be dark soon. Enjoy your pizza party, Sea Dragon."

"Oh, we will. Thanks, kid."

Chris eagerly opened up the sail. Instantly, the wind carried them further out to sea.

"That was not at all what I was expecting," said Chris.

I-doll rubbed his head. "Boy, their bickering gave me such a headache," he cried. "Maybe I should've just let you use your sword after all!"

CHAPTER TWELVE

FIGHT UNDER THE MOONLIGHT

Once again, Tommy woke up face down on the damp floor of Wiz's ship. He peeked around the silent deck, but he couldn't see a thing.

Tommy pushed himself up.

On the tips of his toes, he searched through the dark fog. The only light he had to see came from the faint moonlight above. There was no sign of the Snakey-Chains or Wiz.

Tommy stopped in his tracks.

He covered his ears and bit his lip.

The pizza crates were scattered all over the deck, again!

Tommy stomped over to the pizza crates and began stacking them neatly one by one.

As he placed the final pizza crate on top of the perfectly straight stack, Tommy's eyes lit up with an idea.

Maybe, he could leave a trail of pizza crates in the sea? Tommy thought to himself.

He picked up all of the pizza crates and carried them to the side of the boat.

Leaning over the side, Tommy couldn't see anything through the fog, but he could hear the ocean waves knocking on the boat.

Tommy grabbed one pizza crates and tossed it over. He watched it disappear into the fog. *Splash!*

Tommy laughed. That was actually kind of fun.

He grabbed another pizza crate and threw it overboard. Again, Tommy laughed as he heard it splash in the ocean.

Tommy tossed a third crate over the side.

Clunk! "Ouch!" cried a familiar voice in the fog below. "What the dragon farts was that?"

Another familiar voice giggled.

"Bahaha! Boy, you just got hit in the head with a pizza crate!"

Tommy smiled and jumped with excitement.

"Tommy, is that you up there?" I-doll asked.

"Tommy," Chris whispered loudly, "if you're up there, toss down some rope or something."

Tommy rushed around looking for rope.

He stopped in front of the steamy cauldron and noticed rope lying next to it. Tommy curiously looked around. He didn't remember the rope being there before.

Tommy shrugged. He grabbed the heavy rope and threw one end over the side to his brother and I-doll.

Clunk! "Ouch! Brother, stop dropping things on my head!" Chris cried.

"Boy, quit your crying," I-doll told Chris. "You're wearing a helmet!"

Planting his bare feet into the damp floor, Tommy grasped the rope as Chris and I-doll climbed up.

But Tommy felt they were taking too long to climb. With all his might, Tommy bent his knees and jumped backwards.

Chris and I-doll screamed as they were yanked up and over the side of the boat.

Crash! They landed on top of Tommy.

All three of them groaned and cried.

"Oh, Tommy, that's gonna' leave a mark." Chris cried, rubbing his elbow.

I-doll popped his head out from underneath Chris's bum. "Are you kidding me, boy?" he yelled. "How'd I end up underneath you? It stinks under there!"

Tommy jumped to his feet and helped Chris and I-doll up. He gave them both a giant, tight hug.

"Brother, so glad you're alright," Chris told Tommy.

I-doll hopped up on Tommy's shoulder and squeezed Tommy's face with his arms. "Boy, I'm so sorry. I should've been with you," I-doll said. "I've missed you. By the way, this hug is also from your mother."

Grinning ear to ear, Tommy gave I-doll a tiny high-five.

"So, where's this wizard at?" Chris asked as he pulled out his cool sword. "I want to have a little chat with him."

"Chris, we have Tommy," said I-doll. "I think we should get out of here, quick. We don't need to go looking for more trouble."

With a smirk on his face, Chris tightened the grip around his sword. "Oh, it won't take long."

Tommy quickly pulled the white rock out of his pocket and started drawing on the deck.

Chris and I-doll watched closely.

Tommy drew the three bullies from school, Wiz the wizard, the sick Sea Dragon, and what looked like a stone.

Tommy almost forgot about something – the Snakey-Chains – he drew those too.

"Is that a stone? A Dragon Stone?" I-doll asked. "And, are those the chain snakes? Or what did the Sea Dragon call them?"

Chains clanged and rattled behind the three of them.

"Snakey-Chains!" Chris shouted.

"Jumping pizzas!" I-doll screamed as the Snakey-Chains slithered out of the fog.

Tommy snatched I-doll from his shoulder and ran off.

"Tommy, what are you doing? We have to help your brother!" cried I-doll.

"Finally," Chris said. He held his new sword over his head. "Let's see what my cool sword can do."

But before Chris could swing his cool sword, a Snakey-Chain from behind knocked him to the floor.

The sword flew out of his hands and bounced into the thick fog.

Chris fell hard on his back.

"Oh, c'mon!" Chris yelled, slamming his fist on the deck. He pushed himself up. "I guess I'll have to do this the old-fashioned way." Chris jumped on top of one of the Snakey-Chains and tried wrestling it to the ground.

Two more Snakey-Chains slithered closer, snapping their teeth.

Tommy stopped in front of the pizza crates with I-doll in his hand. He pulled out the bottom crate, threw the lid open, and tossed I-doll inside.

Splat! I-doll landed on top a cheese pizza.

"Tommy, boy, what are you doing?" I-doll asked, wiping cheese from his face. "This isn't the time for a pizza party!"

Tommy slammed the pizza crate shut and quickly stacked the other pizza crates on top.

He went to go help his brother, but Tommy's stomach growled angrily. So, he grabbed a slice of cheese pizza from the top crate – and one for his brother.

"These Snakey-Chains aren't so tough," Chris said with three Snakey-Chains wrapped in his arms. "I could wrestle them in my sleep!"

And then came Tommy with a whole slice of pizza in his mouth.

Tommy handed Chris a slice.

"Tommy! Does this look like we're having a pizza party right now?" Chris yelled.

Tommy swallowed the slice of pizza, and again, he tried to offer his brother the other slice.

"Brother! Behind you!" Chris shouted.

Two more Snakey-Chains slithered out of the fog, snapping at Tommy.

Tommy dropped the slice of pizza and wrestled the Snakey-Chains to the ground while Chris continued bear-hugging the others.

With his thick hands, Tommy grabbed the head and neck of a Snakey-Chain and twisted.

Snap! The head of the Snakey-Chain popped right off.

"Holy dragon strength, Tommy!" Chris shouted. "You snapped its head right off!"

With his thick hands, Chris did the same thing and popped the head off a Snakey-Chain.

Tommy snapped another head off.

"No more games!" a voice shouted from the fog.

Tommy and Chris spun around.

Wiz burst through the fog with more Snakey-Chains slithering and hissing behind him.

CHAPTER THIRTEEN

I-DOLL IN A PIZZA BLANKET

The Snakey-Chains zipped through the fog and wrapped up Tommy and Chris.

"Ugh, there's too many of them! I can't get free!" Chris cried.

Tommy didn't even try to fight it. He'd been wrapped up by the Snakey-Chains before.

Chris glared at the approaching wizard.

"Foolish boy," Wiz spoke to Chris. "You blindly jumped onto my ship with nothing but a sword and a little wooden doll." Wiz searched around the deck for I-doll and turned back to Chris. "You've crossed a short bridge from bravery to stupidity."

"I once met a troll that lived under a bridge," said Chris as he tried to break free from the Snakey-Chains. "Happiest troll I've ever met."

Wiz sighed. "That's not what I... grrr."

"Now, who are you and why did you take my brother?" Chris shouted.

"I am Wiz, and soon, I will be the most powerful wizard in the land and sea."

Chris burst into laughter. "Wait, are you serious? Your name's Wiz?" Chris asked, giggling.

Wiz cringed. "Uh – yes?" he said. "It's short for wizard. What's wrong with it?"

Chris couldn't stop laughing. "Oh, nothing. It's really a perfect name for you," he said. "Carry on. You were just about to tell me why you dragged my brother out here into the Sea of Dragons?"

"Well, if it's not obvious by now," Wiz spoke with an evil chuckle. "I was never after Tommy or you."

Tommy's heart stopped. He peeked over at the pizza crates where I-doll was hiding.

"Not us?" Chris asked.

Wiz stepped in front of Tommy.

Tommy kept his head down as to not give away any hints of I-doll's whereabouts.

"You may not talk, Tommy, but your eyes speak for you," said Wiz. "Where did you hide him?"

Tommy couldn't help himself. His shaking eyes pointed over to the pizza crates.

The wizard smiled and cheerfully hopped over to the pizzas.

Wiz yelled at a couple of seagulls trying to get into the top pizza crate. "Get out of my way, annoying birds!"

Tommy's face sank as he watched Wiz open the top crate.

"Cheese," Wiz looked down at the pizza inside. "Boring." He threw the crate over the side of the ship and opened the next one.

"Oh, pineapple pizza!" Wiz jumped. "Now, that's some good pizza right there. We'll save that one." Wiz set the pizza crate to the side.

Tommy and Chris looked at each other with disgust.

Chris turned his head away. "Ugh, I think I just threw up in my mouth a little," he said. "Of course, you like pineapple pizza. Gross!"

Wiz went through the pizza crates till he got to the last one on the bottom.

"I guess, what I'm really craving," Wiz said as he slowly opened the crate, "is a little slice of I-doll."

Inside the crate, I-doll looked up at Wiz while rubbing cheese and pizza sauce all over himself.

"Oh, hello there," said I-doll. "Don't mind me. I'm just rubbing sauce on my knees. They're sore. It's been a long day. What time is it? It must be late. Well, I must be getting to sleep." I-doll pulled a couple of slices of pizza over him like a blanket.

"Long time no see, I-doll," Wiz said.

I-doll peeked out from under the pizzas. "Sorry, wizard, do I know you?" he asked.

Wiz snatched I-doll from the pizza crate. "I brought you to life, I-doll."

I-doll, Tommy, and Chris looked at each other with wide eyes.

"What are you talking about, Wiz?" Chris asked. "Our father made I-doll himself. He made I-doll to help Tommy communicate."

Tommy thought back to the first time he held I-doll. He couldn't remember much. Tommy couldn't even walk yet. All he remembered was waking up with I-doll in his arms.

"Your father made him – yes," Wiz explained. "But your father travelled far to me that rainy night. He gave me all of his gold. And with magic, I brought I-doll to life. Little did I know then, how powerful and rare that magic really was."

"You're the wizard who brought me to life?" I-doll screeched. "I thought your beard would be longer. But the hat is perfect."

With all his strength, Tommy tried to break free as two more Snakey-Chains slithered up next to Wiz and I-doll.

"Wait," said Chris. "What powerful magic are you talking about?"

Wiz chuckled as he handed I-doll over to the Snakey-Chains. "Real magic," he said with an evil smile.

I-doll shouted as the Snakey-Chains sank their sharp teeth into him. "Hey! Put me down!" he screamed. "You're going to break-" *Snap!*

Tommy and Chris watched in horror as the Snakey-Chains snapped I-doll's body in half.

"No!" Chris yelled, trying to break free from the chains.

Tommy showed no emotions - his mind frozen – his body heavier than a mountain.

Inside of I-doll's quiet body laid a green stone.

Wiz carefully picked it up with the tips of his fingers and admired every detail of the glowing stone.

"The Earth Stone," Wiz said with glowing eyes. "It's perfect. More beautiful than I remember."

"What the dragons is wrong with you!" Chris yelled with watery eyes. "How could you do that? He was our friend! He was family!"

"Real magic sometimes requires real sacrifice," said Wiz. "As a wizard, it's my duty to study the Dragon Stones and their magic. And I wasn't going to let a mighty Dragon Stone waste away inside this annoying doll."

Wiz tossed I-doll away like trash.

Tommy closed his eyes as I-doll's broken body thudded on the deck.

Wiz held up the green Dragon Stone to Chris's face. "This is an Earth Stone," he said. "I must know how powerful it is. What more it can do. I must test it."

Wiz's eyes lit up with an idea. "Hmm. We need a testing area," he said. "Maybe... an island? An island would be perfect."

Tommy's eyes shot open. *An island?* he wondered.

Wiz turned to Tommy with the Earth Stone snuggled between his fingers. "You helped me get the Earth Stone, Tommy," he said. "Now, I will help you. Let's go pay a little visit to those bullies of yours."

"You're a monster!" Chris cried.

"I'm not a monster!" Wiz snapped at Chris as he put the Earth Stone inside his cloak, next to the Water Stone. "Your father was kind to me. Out of respect to him, I will let you live."

One of the Snakey-Chains picked up Chris's cool sword and brought it to Wiz.

"But I'm going to keep the sword," Wiz said. "It's got a nice touch of magic to it."

"Oh, c'mon!" Chris yelled as the Snakey-Chains dragged him to the edge of the ship and tossed him over the side.

Chris landed hard on his head in the tiny, leaking boat. *Thud!*

Chris felt dizzy. His eyes shut and he

passed out.

Still frozen and feeling lost, Tommy watched Wiz's gangly hand pick up I-doll's body.

Wiz handed I-doll to Tommy. "I was going to use it as firewood," said Wiz. "But, I'm in such a great mood tonight. I'll let you hold onto him."

Tommy squeezed out a hand between the Snakey-Chains and took I-doll from him.

I-doll's body felt cold and heavy.

"I know how you feel, Tommy," said Wiz. "But you'll feel better later. Your school's not far from here. We'll teach those bullies a lesson, and I will show you what the Dragon Stones can do."

CHAPTER FOURTEEN

ANNOYING BIRDS

In the middle of the dark sea, Chris laid passed out in his tiny boat. The air was cold and quiet with only the faint light of the moon peeking through the clouds above.

Two Sea Dragons popped their heads out of the calm water and peeked inside the boat with their yellow eyes.

"Patty, look. It's that smelly boy from earlier," said Joey the Sea Dragon.

"Keep your voice down," snapped Patty the Sea Dragon. "That wizard might still be around."

"You think he's alright?" asked Joey the Sea Dragon.

"I don't know. Let's push him away from here before Brother Joey eats him," said Patty.

They nodded in agreement and pushed Chris and the tiny boat out of the Sea of Dragons.

●●●

Aboard his ship, The Pizza Pirate finished fixing the sails that were damaged by the Snakey-Chains.

"Yarr', that oughta' do it. She's ready to sail again, boys!" The Pizza Pirate shouted to his crew. "Light up the oven. It's pizza time!"

"Hooray!" the crew yelled.

"Excuse me, pirate?" came a large voice from the sea.

The Pizza Pirate spun around and drew his sword.

It was Joey the Sea Dragon with the morning sun shining behind him.

"Sea Dragon! Be gone with ye'!" The Pizza Pirate yelled. "Take your slimy, big-nosed face outta' here before I cut ye' flippers right off!"

"Hey, relax, pirate," said Joey the Sea Dragon. "This boy needs help."

Joey the Sea Dragon lifted his tail and dumped the tiny, leaking boat onto the

"Oh, dragon farts," Chris cried as he slowly crawled out of the boat. "My head is spinning like crazy."

"Mother's spicy sausage! Chris, are ye' alright, nephy'?" The Pizza Pirate asked as he helped Chris up to his feet.

Chris fixed his helmet so he could see better. "Uncle, I think so," he said, taking a moment to collect his thoughts. "Actually, no – no, I'm not."

"Sorry to jump in here," said Joey the Sea Dragon, clearing his throat. "You wouldn't happen to have any pizzas I can take back to the Sea of Dragons, would you?"

"Yarr'," The Pizza Pirate grumbled, rolling his one eye. He snapped his fingers at his crew. "Boys, get the dragon some pizzas, to go!"

Chris jumped back into the boat to get Tommy's shield. Behind him, Joey the Sea Dragon took a tall stack of pizzas from the crew and swam out to sea.

Chris kicked the side of the boat. "Bearded dragons!" he yelled. "He did take my sword. I thought it was a bad dream. I thought maybe it was all a bad dream."

"Yarr'! What happened out there? Where be Tommy?" The Pizza Pirate asked.

"Wiz still has him – the wizard," Chris said. "I messed up, uncle."

"What ye' mean, boy?"

"We lost I-doll," Chris said, staring

down at the boat.

"What? How?" The Pizza Pirate cried as his one good eye nearly popped right out.

"It's my fault," said Chris. His eyes teared up. "The wizard – he broke I-doll. There was a Dragon Stone inside him."

"Chunky Cheeses!" Uncle Rick gasped. "A Dragon Stone? Inside of I-doll this whole time?"

"I shouldn't have brought I-doll with me. What was I thinking?" Chris kicked the tiny boat again.

"Nonsense," The Pizza Pirate told Chris. "Ye' was brave. I-doll was brave. Ye' did the right thing."

Chris nodded.

"If we get the Dragon Stone back, can we bring I-doll back?" The Pizza Pirate asked.

"I'm not sure. Maybe." Chris shrugged. "It's an Earth Stone. It's like I-doll's heart, I think."

"Well, where did the wizard take Tommy?" The Pizza Pirate asked.

Chris scratched his chin in deep thought.

"Oh, yes! I remember!" Chris cried out. "He's going to Tommy's school to use the Dragon Stone on some bullies. Tommy *was* being bullied at school. I think that's why he tackled a kid."

"We have to get to the island and stop him!" The Pizza Pirate shouted.

"I don't know if we can," Chris said,

throwing his arms up in the air. "Wiz took my sword, and he has those Snakey-Chains guarding him. We need some kind of distraction."

Splash! A mermaid jumped up to the side of the ship with a bottle in her hand.

"Chris!" the shiny mermaid yelled. "I've been looking all over for you. I have a message for you."

"A message?" Chris asked, taking the bottle from the mermaid. He opened it up and began reading the letter.

Chris giggled.

"What is it, boy?" The Pizza Pirate asked.

"It's from the princess," said Chris. "She wrote me a letter to tell me that she tried pineapple pizza, and she hated it."

"Well then, lad. She's what me would call a keeper!" The Pizza Pirate joked.

Chris crumbled up the letter. "I don't have time for distractions," he mumbled, his face turning bright red.

The Pizza Pirate wobbled over to the mermaid with half a pizza in his mouth. "My beauty," he spoke to the mermaid, "I need you to swim to the island where Tommy's school is, please. You can get there faster. Tell them a wizard is coming their way."

The mermaid smiled and nodded. "I'm on it," she said before diving back into the sea.

Loud shouting and squawking

screeched across the deck.

Chris shot around to see the crewmen chasing away a bunch of seagulls trying to steal crates of pizzas.

"Annoying birds," Chris mumbled. But then, his face lit up with a delicious idea. "The princess hates pineapple pizza," he whispered to himself with a smile on his face. "But I know someone who loves it."

Chris turned to The Pizza Pirate. "Uncle, the princess gave me an idea!" he shouted. "Can you make the most delicious and nose-tingling pineapple pizza ever?"

"Yarr'! Why would ye' want me to do such a horrible thing?" The Pizza Pirate asked, disgusted.

Chris stretched up to his uncle and whispered something into his ear.

"Aye," said The Pizza Pirate, nodding with a big smile. "A fine plan that be, nephy'."

CHAPTER FIFTEEN

REAL MAGIC

Tommy wiggled and kicked, trying to break free from the Snakey-Chains. He grew cranky and tired, and he was fed up.

"There it is – your school." Wiz pointed with excitement.

Clouds slowly filled the sky as Tommy squinted across the sea. His school sat there peacefully next to the misty mountain on the island.

At the beach, the long dock stretched out into the sea. That's where Tommy would get off and walk the rest of the way to school.

Standing at the edge of the dock, a group of knights and soldiers pulled out their shiny swords and shields.

Wiz glared and slammed his staff on the deck. "Looks like someone told them we were coming," Wiz told Tommy.

Tommy felt relieved – a little.

"Not a problem, though," Wiz said. "Perfect, actually." Wiz reached into his cloak and took out the Water Stone.

"Remember the Water Stone we got from the Baby Sea Dragon?" Wiz asked Tommy, holding the Water Stone near the edge of his staff.

Tommy bit his lip and looked away.

"Might as well not let it go to waste," said Wiz with an evil laugh.

Wiz gently placed the Water Stone inside the ring of teeth at the end of his staff.

Glowing much brighter than before, the Water Stone sparked and flashed.

Wiz held his glowing staff high above him. "Perfect!" he shouted.

Tommy tried to look away, but he couldn't help himself as Wiz made his way to the front of the ship.

Wiz pointed his staff at the splashing waves in the sea.

He took a deep breath.

"Rise!" Wiz yelled.

Tommy's jaw dropped.

A massive wall of water rose out of the

sea and raced towards the island.

The knights and soldiers at the dock froze at the sight of the giant wave speeding their way.

All of them dropped their weapons and ran.

But they didn't make it far.

The tall wave of water tore through the dock like stone through paper.

The knights and soldiers screamed as they were helplessly washed away!

With a wide smile on his face, Wiz turned around to a stunned Tommy. "Time for school, Tommy," Wiz said.

●●●

Wiz stepped closer and gazed up at the foggy stone wall surrounding Tommy's school.

Wiz scratched his beard. "Hmm. This is a mighty wall they have built here," he said.

The Snakey-Chains tossed Tommy onto the grassy ground.

Tommy looked up. The sky was gray and dull with puffy clouds hugging the top of the misty mountain.

Not far from him, Tommy could hear the rushing water of the nearby creek where he played with I-doll.

Wiz pondered and stared at the misty mountain. Then he smiled down at Tommy. "Not a problem," Wiz said. "This will be a perfect test for the Earth Stone."

Wiz took out the Water Stone from his staff and swapped it with the Earth Stone in his cloak. "Let's see what I-doll's been hiding from us all these years," said Wiz as he placed the Earth Stone onto the end of his staff.

Just like the Water Stone did before, the Earth Stone sparked and flashed.

"Tommy, do you know about the misty mountain there? Wiz asked. "Did you know that it is a sleeping volcano?"

With the Snakey-Chains slithering around him, Tommy pushed himself up and bit his lip. *What was the volcano going to do?* Tommy thought.

"Let's see if we can wake it up." Wiz held his staff high over his head. He lunged it forward and slammed it into the ground.

"Rise!" Wiz yelled.

But nothing happened this time.

Tommy stared curiously at the misty mountain.

Wiz searched around for any signs of magic.

Suddenly, there was a rumbling near the creek. Birds shot out of trees. Rocks next to Tommy's bare feet trembled.

The Snakey-Chains started to panic.

Wiz smiled with the green Earth Stone sparkling in his eyes.

Crack! Split! The ground ripped apart. Hot air and steam spewed out from the cracks.

A burning hand of lava reached out from ground, and slowly, a monster dripping with fire and lava pulled itself out of the earth.

Tommy couldn't believe it.

Even the Snakey-Chains hid behind stones as the lava monster stomped toward Wiz.

Wiz held up his staff and pointed it to the stone wall around the school. He spoke to the lava monster.

"On the other side of the wall is a school. There are kids in there that need to be taught a lesson," Wiz said. "Destroy it... All of it."

The lava monster looked down at Tommy with bright, orange eyes. Dripping with lava, it turned away and slowly marched toward the wall.

"Smelly dragon farts!" Chris shouted. "Is that a lava monster?"

Chris ran up to Tommy and Wiz with three pizza crates in his arms and Tommy's shield on his back.

The Snakey-Chains slithered in front, hissing and snapping. One of them still carried Chris's cool sword in its mouth.

"Whoa, easy there, Snakey-Chains," Chris said, taking a few steps back. "I come in peace."

Tommy smiled at his brother, but he couldn't get to him – not with the Snakey-Chains between them.

"What are you up to, boy?" Wiz asked, glaring at Chris.

Behind Wiz, the lava monster slowly but surely stomped closer to the wall.

Chris shrugged. "Sorry I'm late to the party," he told Wiz. "I have a peace offering. Three delicious, fresh pineapple pizzas from The Pizza Pirate." Chris winked at Tommy. "And all I want is my brother back."

Wiz licked his lips. His stomach growled like a dragon roaring in a cave. The sweet smell of pineapple and melted cheese tickled his nose.

"Very well." Wiz nodded.

Chris let out a deep breath and handed out the pizza crates to Wiz.

"One more thing," Wiz said. "If we're having a pizza party, we need more guests."

Wiz raised his staff above his head and slammed it into the ground once again.

"Rise!" Wiz shouted.

The earth trembled. The ground split and cracked like shattered glass. Pools of lava formed all around them. And more drooling lava monsters climbed out of the earth.

"Perfect!" Wiz shouted. He turned around and waved his staff at the Snakey-Chains.

The Snakey-Chains let Tommy go. Two others slithered over to Chris and took the pizzas.

Tommy ran to his brother, and together, they watched Wiz go to open the pizza crate.

CHAPTER SIXTEEN

WHAT'S THE PLAN?

Wiz breathed in the delicious smell as he cracked open the pizza crate.

"Oh, this smells delicious."

Bam! Squawk! Squawk! Seagulls burst out of the pizza crates!

Flapping around, the angry birds pecked and jabbed at Wiz.

One of them flew off with his pointy hat.

Wiz panicked. He dropped his staff and ran as the seagulls tried to rip his ears off.

The Snakey-Chains also panicked. They chased after the seagulls. Two of them fell and melted into a pool of lava.

Crushed by the foot of a lava monster, the Snakey-Chain dropped Chris's new sword.

The cool sword bounced on the ground, barely missing a pool of lava.

Chris grabbed Tommy's arm and pointed to the staff surrounded by lava.

"Tommy, remember yesterday when we were pretending the floor was hot lava?" Chris asked.

Tommy nodded. He giggled when he remembered they had broken the breakfast table.

"Well, this is the real deal, brother," Chris told Tommy. "Hop across the lava and grab Wiz's staff. Meet me behind the trees."

Chris adjusted his helmet and tightened the cape around his neck. "I'm going get my sword back."

Chris leapt across pools of lava, dodging and rolling out of the way of the stomping lava monsters. *Jump! Dodge! Jump! Dodge!*

With one last jump, Chris landed face down in the dirt. His shiny, cool sword sparkled in front of him.

"Yes!" Chris shouted. He jumped up and held his sword high above him. "Hey, you know what?" Chris asked his cool sword. "I should come up with a name for you." He scratched his chin for a brief second. "How about, Frosty? That's a fitting name, I think."

Across a river of lava, Tommy landed in front of the staff. He picked it up. He went to take out the Earth Stone, but a lava monster stomped in front of him.

"Brother! I almost forgot!" Chris shouted to Tommy. He took the shield from his back. "Mother made this shield. Catch!"

Chris tossed the shield over the river of lava.

Tommy caught it with one hand and wrapped it tightly around his arm.

The lava monster grew closer.

"Tommy! The shield has an Ice Stone in it! It should work!" Chris yelled.

Tommy planted his feet. He bent his legs, leaned forward, and charged at the lava monster with his shield.

Bam! The lava monster splattered all over the ground.

"Nice!" Chris yelled.

The two brothers hopped across the pools of lava and met up behind a large tree.

"Phew, that was close," Chris told Tommy.

Tommy gave Chris a quick high-five.

The brothers gazed at the glowing Earth Stone at the end of the staff.

With his thick fingers, Tommy slowly pulled the Earth Stone out of the ring of teeth.

"Careful," Chris told Tommy.

Tommy took out I-doll's cold, dry body from his cloak and gently held the Earth Stone near the hole in I-doll's chest.

After taking a deep breath, Tommy slowly placed the Earth Stone inside I-doll.

Pop! Tommy and Chris covered their eyes from a bright flash.

"Ouch!" I-doll cried.

I-doll stood up in Tommy's flat hands.

"Wait, where am I?" I-doll asked, looking up into Tommy's watery eyes. "Tommy boy!"

Tommy squeezed I-doll against his face. I-doll's wooden body felt smooth and warm again.

"Thank you, boy," I-doll told Tommy. He sniffed the air. "What's that smell?"

I-doll turned around to see Chris. "Oh, it's you," I-doll joked.

Chris chuckled and gave I-doll a tiny high-five. "I'm glad you're back, toothpick."

"So, uh, what I miss?" I-doll asked, looking around.

Chris scratched his chin and took a deep breath. "Well, after Wiz broke you and took the Dragon Stone that's inside you, he dragged Tommy to his school and used it to bring a bunch of lava monsters to life. And now they're about to destroy the school and everyone in it."

"There's a what inside me?" I-doll cried.

"We'll go over it later," Chris told I-doll.

Tommy, Chris, and I-doll peeked

around the wide tree trunk.

The area was bubbling with steaming lava, with only bits and pieces of land to jump on.

The army of lava monsters stomped toward the school, a few of them already climbing up the stone wall.

"I don't see Wiz anywhere," Chris said.

"No, but I see a couple of his Snakey-Chains." I-doll cringed.

Two Snakey-Chains slithered helplessly across the pools of lava.

"Now what?" Chris asked. "There's no way we can stop all of them." He looked at his sword, Frosty, with an idea. "What if we used one of the Ice Stones from our weapons to freeze the lava monsters!"

Tommy shook his head.

"Why not, brother?"

"Tommy's right," said I-doll. "The wizard's staff can only control elements. There's no ice around here to control."

Holding the staff, Tommy remembered the Water Stone he had snuck into his pocket. He yanked it out and gently placed it inside the ring of teeth.

The Water Stone sparked and flashed at the end of the staff.

Chris and I-doll jumped.

"Boy, what is that?" I-doll cried.

"Is that another Dragon Stone?" Chris asked.

Tommy leaned around the tree and pointed to the creek on the other side of the army of lava monsters.

"It's a Water Stone," said I-doll. "If we can get to that creek, maybe we can use the water to wash away this mess!"

Tommy nodded.

Chris took a good look at the creek. "It'll take too long to go around," he said, scratching his chin. "Here's the plan – I'll distract the lava monsters while you two make a run for the creek."

"Sounds good to me!" I-doll shouted as he hopped up onto Tommy's shoulder. "I'm not going anywhere near those lava monsters!"

Chris grabbed Tommy's shoulder and looked him in the eyes. "Brother, do your magic."

Tommy smiled and put his shield over his heart – a sign of courage.

"Boys, let's put our fists together," I-doll told Tommy and Chris as he stretched his tiny fist out.

"What are you doing?" Chris asked.

"We're a team," said I-doll. "Let's put our fists together. It's something I thought of. Might be fun!"

Tommy and Chris slowly touched their dirty fists to I-doll's.

"This is weird," Chris said.

Tommy shrugged.

"Go team!" I-doll yelled.

"How about, go knights!" Chris said.

Tommy giggled.

I-doll nodded. "Yes, boy. That's much

better."

Chris laughed. "Now, let's go chop up some lava monsters."

CHAPTER SEVENTEEN

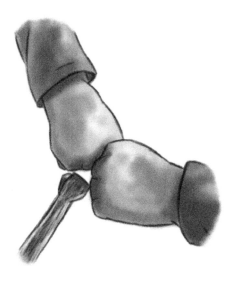

WE'RE A TEAM

Chris charged at the army of lava monsters with Frosty clung in his hands. He jumped at the nearest monster and swung as hard as he could. *Slash!*

The lava monster groaned as it split in half and splattered all over the ground.

With his jaw to the floor, Chris held Frosty high above him. "Yes!" he shouted. "Frosty! That... was... so... cool!"

Another lava monster lunged at Chris from behind!

"Ah!" Chris ducked under its steaming

arms and rolled around it. He swung his sword again and cut the lava monster's legs clean off. "Ha-ha! It's like cutting through butter!" Chris shouted. "Nice work, mother!"

The ground beneath Chris exploded and knocked him to the ground.

A lava monster burst through. It growled at Chris but turned away and stomped toward the school.

The lava monsters climbing the wall were nearly to the top.

Chris gasped. "Oh, dragon farts. Brother! Hurry!" Chris shouted over to Tommy as he chopped off the head of a lava monster. "They're almost over the wall!"

Tommy leapt across a puddle of lava onto some soft grass. He tightened the shield around his hand and gripped the staff in the other. He jumped again. Coughing, Tommy stopped to catch his breath. He struggled to see through all of the steam and smoke pouring from the cracks in the ground.

"Oh, boy. This is hot," I-doll cried, hanging on tightly to Tommy's shoulder.

Then I-doll heard a familiar and awful sound.

A slithering sound.

Two Snakey-Chains hissed at Tommy and I-doll.

Tommy raised his shield.

I-doll threw his tiny arms in the air and

yelled, "I give up!" He hopped off of Tommy's shoulder and landed in front of the Snakey-Chains. "Catch me if you can!" he yelled at the Snakey-Chains before disappearing into the smoke.

The Snakey-Chains chased after I-doll.

"Hurry, boy!" I-doll shouted to Tommy.

Tommy rubbed the sweat from his forehead with the end of his cloak. He took a deep breath and dashed toward the creek.

He was nearly there. Tommy could hear the running water and see the sparkling splashes through the smoke.

Tommy stopped.

Wiz jumped in front of him.

Covered in seagull dung, Wiz lunged at Tommy with crazy eyes and grabbed the staff in Tommy's hand.

But Tommy didn't let go.

"Give me my staff!" Wiz screamed. "I won't let you take my magic away from me!"

Tommy pulled back, trying to break free from Wiz's grasp.

Crack! The ground split open.

A steaming lava hand reached out and grabbed Wiz's foot.

"Aaahh!" Wiz screamed in pain. He let go of the staff.

The lava monster started to drag Wiz toward a pool of lava.

Tommy ran for the creek.

But then he stopped.

"Help!" Wiz shouted. "Somebody, please, help me!"

Tommy charged at the lava monster and slammed his shield down on its arm.

The lava monster let go and disappeared back into the earth.

Wiz rolled over and tried to sooth his burnt leg. He looked at Tommy but said nothing.

Tommy ran and leapt into the creek. The cold water rushed through his toes as he made his way into the middle of the splashing water.

Tommy threw his shield away and lifted the staff above his head. He lunged forward and splashed the end of it into the water.

But the Water Stone did nothing.

Tommy bit his lip and looked around for answers. *Why wasn't it working?* he wondered.

Then he remembered.

Wiz spoke 'rise' when he used the staff.

Tommy moved his lips around. He had only spoken one word in his whole life and it wasn't 'rise'.

Across the pools of lava, Chris hacked and slashed at the lava monsters, but there were too many of them.

A lava monster smacked the cool sword from Chris's hands and stomped toward the boy.

"Brother, now would be a good time," Chris whispered.

I-doll hopped through the smoke. He rolled, dodged and climbed. But he could run no more.

I-doll was stuck between a boulder and two Snakey-Chains.

"Oh, boy," I-doll cried.

Tommy moved his lips and tongue.

He focused, closed his eyes, and breathed.

"R- R- Ri- Rise," Tommy spoke softly.

The water climbed.

The creek grew larger.

A giant wave rose above the trees.

Tommy laughed with relief as the water lunged forward at the army of lava monsters.

Chris laughed. He rolled through the legs of a lava monster and ran to I-doll. Leaping over the Snakey-Chains, Chris snagged I-doll and quickly climbed up a tree.

The water rushed over the lava and smoke.

The lava monsters turned to lava rock and crumbled to the ground.

Steam poured out of the cracks in the earth as water filled them up.

The waves splashed up the stone wall and ate up the lava monsters near the top.

The water began to settle, and the lava and its monsters were gone.

Wiz rolled over, soaking wet. He tried to stand but couldn't with his burnt foot. He looked up.

Tommy, Chris, and I-doll stood there proudly.

Chris lifted his sword and held the sharp edge to Wiz's neck.

"Go ahead, boy," Wiz told Chris. "Do it. Strike me down. Show your brother what being a knight is all about."

CHAPTER EIGHTEEN

KNIGHTS

With the blade of his sword pointed at Wiz's neck, Chris was ready to teach the wizard a lesson. But then he glanced at his brother.

Tommy put his hand over his heart – a signal for love and courage.

Chris smiled.

"You know what?" Chris asked.

Wiz looked up with curious eyes.

"We've been so worried about being good examples for Tommy," Chris said. "When actually, we could learn a thing or two from him."

Tommy smiled while I-doll patted him on the head.

Chris lowered his sword and put it away. "You're going into the dungeons," he told Wiz, "for a long time."

Wiz rolled over and gave up.

Tommy ran and gave Chris a loud high-five. He felt proud. Tommy was tired and hungry, but he felt proud.

Everything was perfect again... almost.

●●●

Tommy returned to school the next day. Everything felt the same as before, as if no one had a clue that the school was nearly melted away by an army of lava monsters.

At break time, Tommy ran to his favorite tree in the corner of the courtyard. Laying between the blades of grass, a torn page from his favorite wizard book flapped in the wind.

Tommy decided he was done with wizards and maybe should find a new favorite book. *There was that one book about elves that seemed interesting.*

Suddenly, three tall shadows hovered above Tommy.

"Hey there, dummy!" Trent squealed. "I can't believe you showed your stupid face here again, after what you did yesterday!"

Tommy's stomach and fists tightened like before.

But Tommy noticed something different.

Trent's goons, Boon and Foon, weren't giggling and laughing like the last time.

"You almost got us all killed!" Trent screamed in Tommy's face. "Because of you, an army of lava monsters almost wiped us away!"

Trent shoved Tommy.

Tommy planted his feet into the grass, trying very hard not to tackle Trent again.

"Do it, dummy!" Trent squealed. "I know you want to. Knock me to the ground. They'll never let you into this school again, and there's not a darn thing you can say about it."

Boon and Foon whispered to each other in the back.

Tommy dug his feet deeper into the grass. He lifted his arms... and crossed them over his chest.

Tommy stood there like a rock.

"Heh, tough guy now, huh?" Trent snorted. "Well, if you're not gonna' do anything... then I'll just pound you into the ground and make up a story later."

Grunting, Trent raised his fat fist up high and went to swing.

"No!" Boon and Foon yelled.

Tommy jumped with surprise as Boon and Foon hopped in front of him.

Trent backed away. "Wha– what? What are you two doing?" he cried.

"This is wrong!" Boon shouted.

"Yeah, Tommy saved us yesterday. We wouldn't be here if it wasn't for him," Foon snapped.

"But... he's a dummy," Trent cried.

"No, you're the dummy." Boon pointed at Trent.

Tommy smiled at his new friends. He didn't expect this.

Trent threw his arms up in the air. "Fine! You're all dummies!" he squealed. "I'm getting out of here!" Trent tried to stomp away but bumped into somebody.

Trent looked up.

It was their teacher, Miss Egghead.

"Oh, you're not going anywhere!" Miss Egghead snapped at Trent. "I heard the whole thing."

Trent cried and kicked like a baby as Miss Egghead dragged him through the grass.

The teacher leaned down and placed her hand on Tommy's shoulder. "I owe you an apology, Tommy," said Miss Egghead. "I knew something wasn't right here. You're a good kid. Don't ever be afraid to tell me something. Draw it. Show it. However you need to."

Tommy smiled and blushed a little.

"Oh, and I have a surprise for you, Tommy," Miss Egghead added as she dragged Trent away.

Behind Miss Egghead, stood Chris and I-doll. They rushed over to Tommy.

I-doll carried a crate of pizza over his head.

Tommy jumped with joy.

"Brother, were you surprised?" Chris asked.

I-doll set the pizza crate in the soft grass and hopped up on Tommy's shoulder.

"Surprise, boy!" I-doll shouted in Tommy's ear.

"My school is still burnt down." Chris shrugged. "So, Uncle Rick dropped us off to have lunch with you."

I-doll giggled with joy. "And, your teacher has decided that I can come to school with you from now on!" he shouted. "She felt it might be for the best."

Tommy smiled and gave I-doll a tiny high-five.

"Let's eat!" Chris yelled as he plopped down in front of the pizza. "I'm starving!"

Tommy went to sit when he noticed Boon and Foon on the other side of the tree. He waved his arm for them to come and eat.

Boon and Foon ran over. "Thanks, Tommy," they said as the two of them grabbed a slice of pizza.

"You know what, boys?" said I-doll. "I might not be able to eat, and maybe this is just the cheesy smell talking, but I'm so proud."

Tommy and Chris looked at each other and rolled their eyes.

"Oh, dragon farts," Chris said, giggling. "The toothpick's getting all sappy on us."

"I'm serious, boy!" I-doll yelled.

"Spreading courage and helping others... that's what being a knight is all about! And one day, you'll both be real knights. I promise!"

Tommy and Chris smiled.

I-doll threw his hands in the air and yelled, "But stop calling me a toothpick!"

Under the shady tree, the heroes laughed and joked as they crammed their mouths with delicious pizza.

IN LOVING MEMORY OF

RICK WOODFORD

ABOUT THE AUTHOR

CHRISTOPHER SR. GREW UP LOVING STORIES OF FANTASY AND SCIENCE-FICTION. AFTER MARRYING HIS BEAUTIFUL WIFE, A DRAGON DELIVERED TO THEM A COUPLE OF BABY BOYS. HE WRITES FOR HIS KIDS, CHRISTOPHER JR. AND THOMAS, AND HE HOPES THAT HIS BOOKS INSPIRE HIS BOYS AND ENTERTAIN KIDS EVERYWHERE.

11135592R00073